Katie Woo's

✽ Neighborhood ✽

Firefighter
Kayla

by Fran Manushkin

illustrated by Laura Zarrin

PICTURE WINDOW BOOKS
a capstone imprint

Katie Woo's Neighborhood is published by Picture Window Books,
an imprint of Capstone.
1710 Roe Crest Drive
North Mankato, Minnesota 56003
www.capstonepub.com

Library of Congress Cataloging-in-Publication Data
Names: Manushkin, Fran, author. | Zarrin, Laura, illustrator.
Title: Firefighter Kayla / by Fran Manushkin; illustrated by Laura Zarrin.
Description: North Mankato, Minnesota : Picture Window Books, a
Capstone imprint, [2021] | Series: Katie Woo's neighborhood | Audience:
Ages 5–7. | Audience: Grades K–1. |
Summary: "JoJo's aunt Kayla is a firefighter. She's teaching Katie's class
about her job. Katie keeps trying to ask Kayla questions, but Kayla has
lots to say before it's question time. If Katie is patient, will she learn what
she really wants to know about firefighters?"-- Provided by publisher.
Identifiers: LCCN 2020035136 (print) | LCCN 2020035137 (ebook) | ISBN
9781515882404 (hardcover) | ISBN 9781515883494 (paperback) | ISBN
9781515891949 (pdf) | ISBN 9781515892915 (kindle edition)
Subjects: CYAC: Fire fighters—Fiction. | Aunts—Fiction. | Chinese
American—Fiction.
Classification: LCC PZ7.M3195 Fi 2021 (print) | LCC PZ7.M3195 (ebook) |
DDC [E]—dc23
LC record available at https://lccn.loc.gov/2020035136
LC ebook record available at https://lccn.loc.gov/2020035137

Designer: Bobbie Nuytten

Table of Contents

Katie's Neighborhood

Police

Library

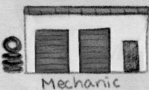
Mechanic

City Hall

Grocery Store

Post Office

School

Chapter 1
A Class Trip

Katie's class was on the

way to visit a fire station.

JoJo's Aunt Kayla worked

there. She was a firefighter.

Katie told JoJo, "I can't

wait to meet her!"

Aunt Kayla welcomed the
class. She asked them right
away, "Do your homes have
smoke detectors?"

"Yes!" yelled everyone.

"Great!" said Aunt Kayla.

Then Aunt Kayla asked them, "What is the first thing to do if there is a fire?"

"That's easy," said Katie. "I would call 911."

"Not yet," said Aunt
Kayla. "First you should get
out of the house. Then you
call 911."

"Oh, right!" said Katie.

"Very right," agreed JoJo.

Katie said, "Can I ask you a question?"

"I'll answer questions later," said Aunt Kayla. "First, I want to tell you about my job."

They walked around
the fire station. Pedro said,
"I don't see a pole to slide
down. That would be fun!"

"Our fire station has only
one floor," said Aunt Kayla.
"We don't need a pole. But
we have a fire dog. Flash is
a lot of fun!"

Chapter 2

More About the Job

"Now I'll show you my gear," said Aunt Kayla. She put on her coat and her helmet and her good, strong boots.

Katie told JoJo, "Your aunt looks so cool!"

"My coat is heavy," said Aunt Kayla. "It protects me from heat and flames."

"Good!" said Katie. "Can I ask my question now?"

"Soon," said Aunt Kayla. "First, I'll show you my fire truck. The siren is very loud! It tells cars to get out of the way. We need to reach the fire fast!"

"Our truck has tall

ladders and long hoses. We

go up the ladders and shoot

water at the fire."

"*Whoooooosh!*" said

Katie and JoJo.

"Now can I ask my question?" said Katie.

"Yes!" Aunt Kayla nodded.

"Now is the perfect time."

Katie said softly, "I am worried about you. Isn't it scary to fight fires?"

"It is," said Aunt Kayla.

"But we are good at doing

our job. We have trained for

a long time."

"Kayla and all the firefighters are a team," said JoJo. "They watch out for each other."

"Good!" Katie smiled.

Chapter 3
A Team

Miss Winkle told Aunt

Kayla, "Thank you for letting

us visit your fire station."

All the kids cheered!

JoJo and Katie and Pedro
walked home with Aunt
Kayla. She asked them,
"Would you like to try on
my gear?"

"For sure!" said Katie.

Aunt Kayla took a photo of JoJo in her coat, Pedro in her boots, and Katie in her helmet.

They felt very cool!

The next day, Katie and JoJo heard a fire siren. They ran out to the porch.

Aunt Kayla's truck was speeding by!

JoJo said, "I'm so proud of my aunt. When I grow up I want to be as brave as her."

"Let's be brave together," said Katie. "We'll be a team."

They shook on it!

Glossary

firefighter (FYR-fye-tur)—a person who is trained to put out fires

fire station (FYR STAY-shuhn)—a building where fire trucks are kept and where firefighters wait until they are called to put out a fire

gear (GEER)—equipment or clothing

helmet (HEL-mit)—a hard hat that protects the head

siren (SYE-ruhn)—a device that makes a loud sound

smoke detector (SMOHK dih-TEK-ter)—a machine that senses smoke and warns people by making loud noises

Katie's Questions

1. What traits make a good firefighter? Would you like to be a firefighter? Why or why not?

2. Katie's class took a field trip to the fire station. Write a paragraph about a field trip you've taken.

3. Draw a picture of Kayla in her fire gear. Then label each of the pieces of gear she is wearing.

4. What did you learn from this story?

5. There are many fire safety rules. Make a poster that shares a rule you know. If you can't think of one, ask an adult for help!

Katie Interviews a Firefighter

Katie: Hello, Ms. Kayla. I'm so happy to talk more about your job today.

Firefighter Kayla: I love talking to children about my job, especially girls. Only about four percent of firefighters in the United States are women. So it is important to reach out to girls and tell them they can do this job too!

Katie: What kind of training did you have to do to become a firefighter?

Firefighter Kayla: Most firefighters are volunteers. They train and pass tests. I am a professional firefighter and get paid for this job. First, I went to a special school. Then I worked with firefighters with experience. I learned some important skills by working with those men and women.

Katie: We saw your gear on the field trip. What other tools do you use on the job?

Firefighter Kayla: We wear face masks, which are attached to air tanks that we carry. The masks help us breathe when we are working in the smoke. We also use thermal cameras. These are special cameras that show people's body heat. That helps us find and rescue people in dark, smoky rooms.

Katie: What's something kids might not know about firefighters?

Firefighter Kayla: Well, we do more than put out fires. We help at car and plane crashes or after a bad storm. We try to help people feel better after something bad happens.

Katie: Thank you for taking such good care of our neighborhood!

Firefighter Kayla: You are very welcome, Katie.

About the Author

Fran Manushkin is the author of Katie
Woo, the highly acclaimed fan-favorite
early reader series, as well as the popular
Pedro series. Her other books include
Happy in Our Skin, *Baby, Come Out!* and

the best-selling board books *Big Girl Panties* and *Big Boy
Underpants*. There is a real Katie Woo: Fran's great-niece,
who doesn't get into trouble like the Katie in the books. Fran
lives in New York City, three blocks from Central Park, where
she can often be found bird-watching and daydreaming. She
writes at her dining room table, without the help of her two
naughty cats, Chaim and Goldy.

About the Illustrator

Laura Zarrin spent her early childhood
in the St. Louis, Missouri, area. There she
explored creeks, woods, and attic closets,
climbed trees, and dug for artifacts in
the backyard, all in preparation for her
future career as an archaeologist. She never
became one, however, because she realized
she's much happier drawing in the comfort of her own home
while watching TV. When she was twelve, her family moved
to the Silicon Valley in California, where she still lives with
her very logical husband and teen sons, and their illogical
dog, Cody.